Purple Bear Books

NEW YORK

The 100th Customer

By Byung-Gyu Kim and K. T. Hao

Illustrated by Giuliano Ferri

TRANSLATED BY ANNIE KUNG

Ben Bear and Chris Croc were about to open a restaurant—a restaurant that sold only two things: mouthwatering pizzas and luscious desserts.

A few minutes before the grand opening an old woman and a little boy pushed open the door and peeked in. Delighted, Ben Bear and Chris Croc rushed to greet their very first customers.

Ben Bear proudly described their special pizzas. "We use only the finest ingredients—wild mushrooms, sweet bell peppers, caviar, prosciutto, even truffles!"

"Which is the least expensive?" asked the woman.

"Price is not the issue, ma'am," replied Ben Bear. "Taste comes first. Tomatoes and olives are the best value—excellent quality at the lowest price!"

"Well, then," said the woman, "one small pizza with tomatoes and olives for my grandson, please."

"And for you?" asked Ben Bear.

"Oh, I'm not at all hungry," the woman replied.

When the pizza was served, the boy turned to his grandmother. "Grandma, are you sure you aren't hungry?"

His grandmother smiled. "I'm sure, dear," she said. "Now eat up before it gets cold."

The boy dug right in and gobbled up the pizza in no time at all. His grandmother smiled with joy to see him so happy.

Ben Bear whispered something to Chris Croc. Suddenly, music filled the room. Ben Bear and Chris Croc sang and danced around the table.

"Congratulations!" declared Ben Bear, placing a second pizza and a fabulous ice-cream sundae on the table. "You, young man, are our 100th customer today and have won free pizza and free dessert!"

Ben Bear and Chris Croc stood happily watching the boy and his grandmother enjoy their free meal together.

"What a wonderful idea, Ben," said Chris Croc, "pretending that boy was our 100th customer."

"Well," Ben Bear agreed, "his grandmother showed me something important today: a full heart is more satisfying than a full stomach."

The next day during the busy lunch hour, Ben Bear happened to look out of the window. He was surprised to see the very same little boy sitting across the street. He had a big pile of pebbles on his right side and a smaller pile on his left. Every time a customer entered the restaurant, the boy would take a pebble from the pile on his right and move it to the pile on the left. If two customers entered the restaurant together, the boy would move two pebbles.

Hmmm . . . thought Ben Bear. He wants to be the 100th customer again, but we have a long way to go. He rushed to the phone and called everyone he knew. "Come now for some free pizza!"

"Fifty-five . . . sixty-six . . ."
It was still a long way from 100.

"Seventy-seven . . . eighty-eight . . ." Finally, the little boy shouted,
"Ninety-nine!" and raced across the street to get in line.

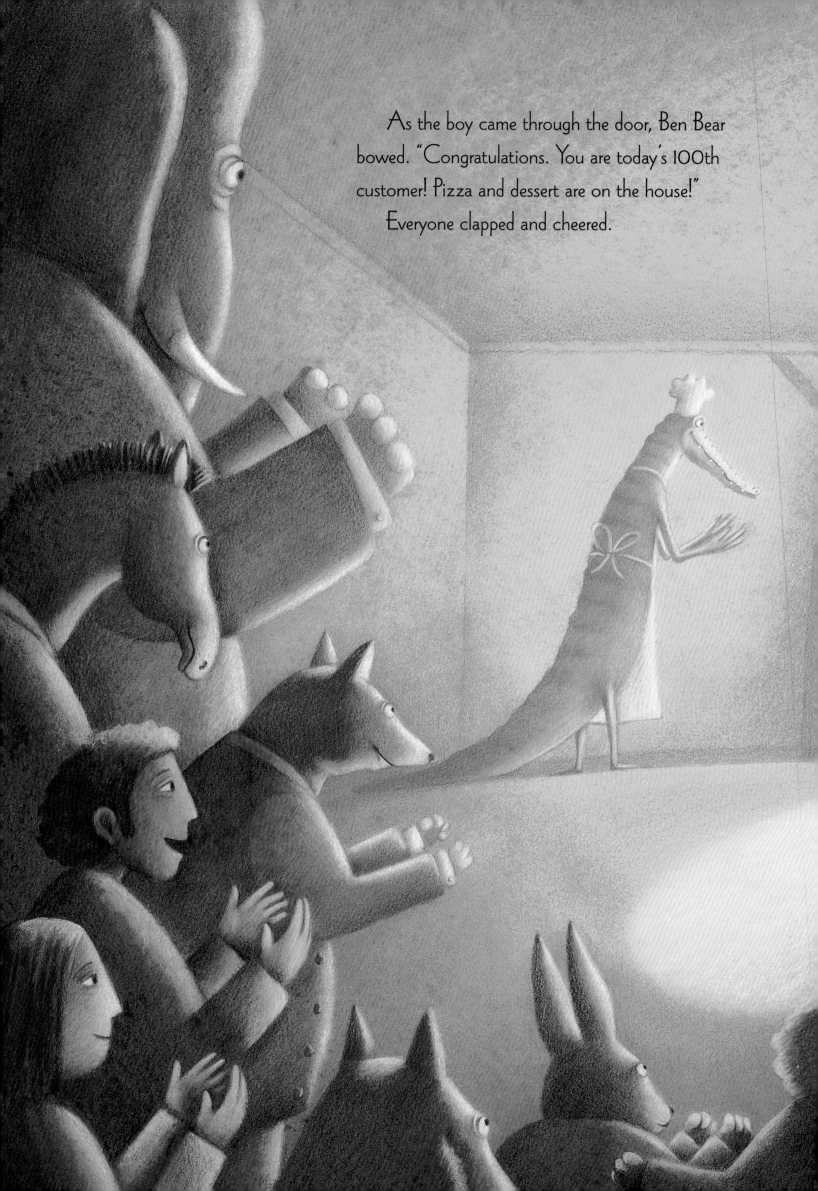

As the boy came through the door, Ben Bear bowed. "Congratulations. You are today's 100th customer! Pizza and dessert are on the house!" Everyone clapped and cheered.

Hurry, hurry! Ben Bear popped a scrumptious pizza into the oven. Chris Croc started work on a luscious dessert. And the little boy raced to the phone to call his grandmother.

Everything was ready and waiting when the grandmother arrived.

"Here, Grandma," said the boy proudly, "a free meal just for you!"

"But you should have some, too," replied his grandmother.

"I'm not at all hungry," said the boy, smiling as he watched his grandmother eat.

"Should we make another free pizza for the boy?" asked Chris Croc.

"Maybe later," Ben Bear replied. "That boy has just learned that a full heart is more satisfying than a full stomach. Let him enjoy his discovery for a while."

Ben Bear and Chris Croc owned a restaurant that served pizzas and desserts AND smiling faces and warm hearts.

The restaurant was a huge success and was crowded every day of the week. Lines of customers snaked out the front door and down the road.

No one minded the wait, they all wanted to be the 100th customer.

Illustrations copyright © 2004 by Giuliano Ferri
Original text copyright © by Byung-Gyu Kim
Rewritten text copyright © 2004 by K. T. Hao
English translation copyright © 2005 by Purple Bear Books Inc.

First published in Taiwan in 2004 by Grimm Press
First English-language edition published in 2005 by Purple Bear Books Inc., New York
For more information about our books visit our website, purplebearbooks.com

Library of Congress Cataloging-in-Publication Data is available.
This edition prepared by Cheshire Studio.

ISBN 1-933327-03-0 (trade edition)
1 3 5 7 9 TE 10 8 6 4 2
ISBN 1-933327-07-3 (library edition)
1 3 5 7 9 LE 10 8 6 4 2
Printed in Taiwan